Down the Drain

Contents

Written by Clare Helen Welsh

Collins

What are drains?

Drains are designed to carry water and other liquids. Liquids we have finished with go down the drain.

storm drain

Storm drains keep water off the streets.

Have you seen these drains?

point drain

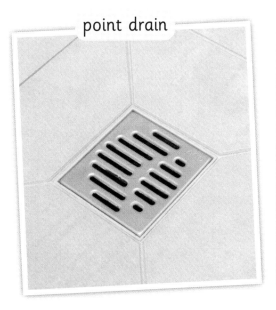

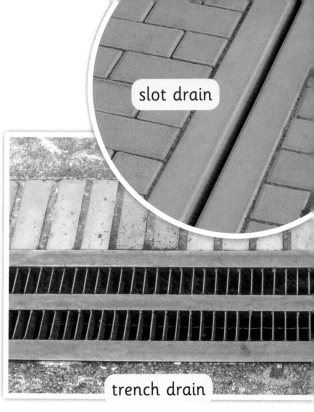

slot drain

trench drain

Did you know?

Drains can be above ground, too.

Guttering runs along the tops of houses and connects to downspouts, which drain rainwater to the ground.

downspouts

Where do pipes go?

Drainpipes carry water underground to a network of tunnels known as sewers.

Water from sinks, toilets, baths, showers and dishwashers contains germs and chemicals. Sewer pipes take this waste water to be cleaned so that it can be put back into rivers safely.

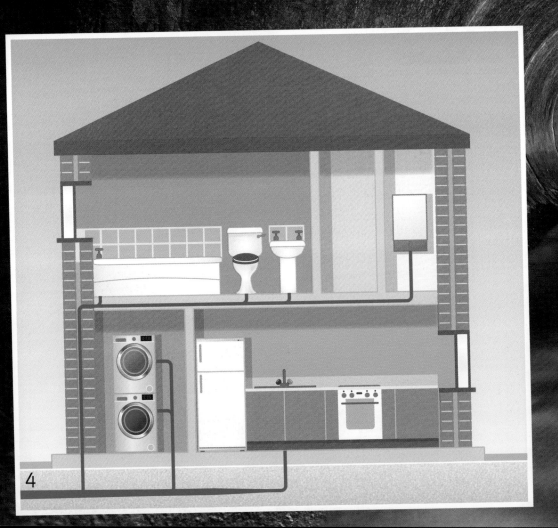

sewer pipe

Did you know?

Storm drains carry rainwater directly into rivers.

Don't pour waste water into storm drains as this can cause pollution in rivers.

storm drain tunnel

How is water cleaned?

Water is filtered and cleaned in a place called a treatment plant.

treatment plant

First, it enters a trap specially designed to take out rubble picked up in the sewers.

grit trap

Screening is a process that gets rid of any large objects.

screening

Items that should never go down a drain

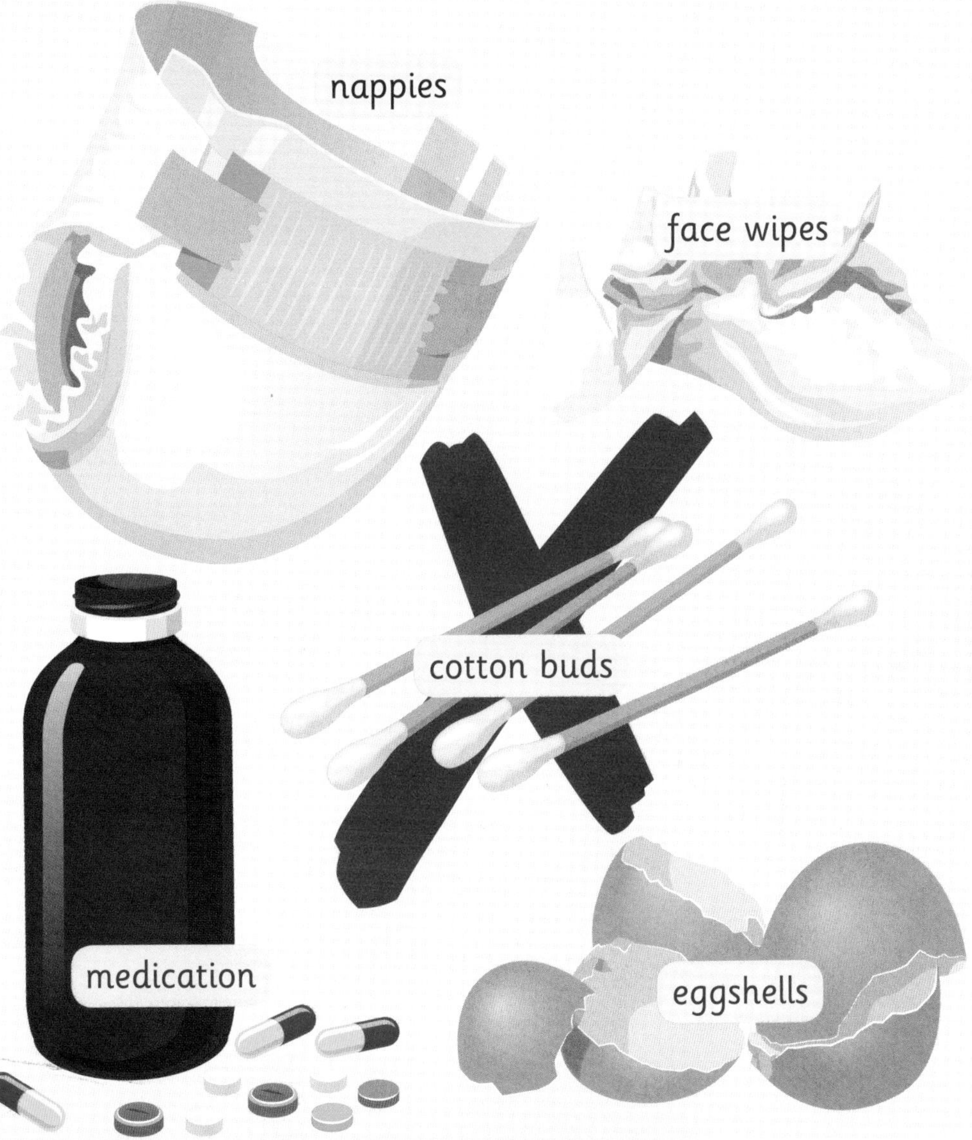

nappies

face wipes

cotton buds

medication

eggshells

Waste water then goes into a settlement tank where the solids eventually sink and form a sludge.

settlement tank

solids

The tank's special design allows clean water to flow over the wall and into the next stage.

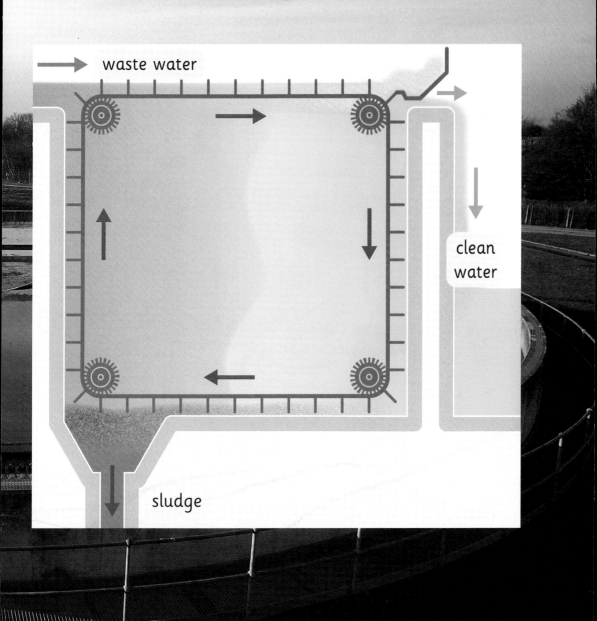

The water still contains dangerous germs. To make the water safe, special germs are added.

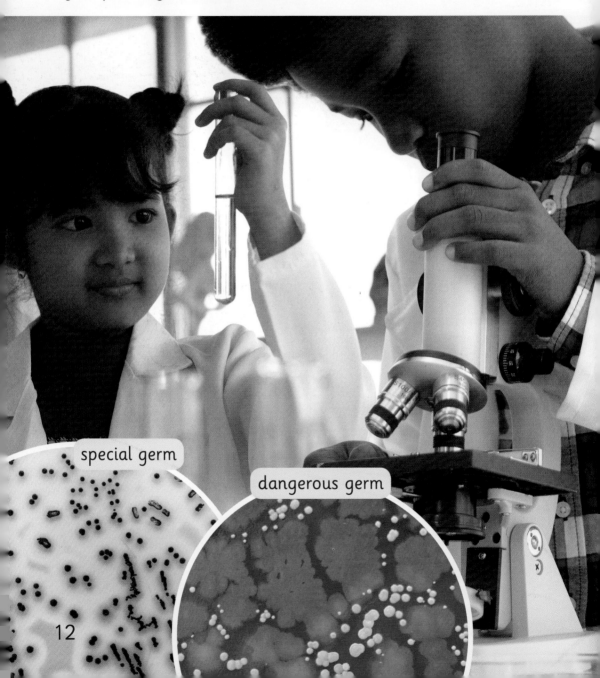

special germ

dangerous germ

The special germs feed on the dangerous germs and get rid of them.

Did you know?
Rivers need clean water to stay healthy.

13

What happens to the sludge?

Sludge from treatment plants is recycled into fertiliser.

Did you know?

Sludge fertiliser is known as "cake".

Sludge is also used in the generation of electricity.

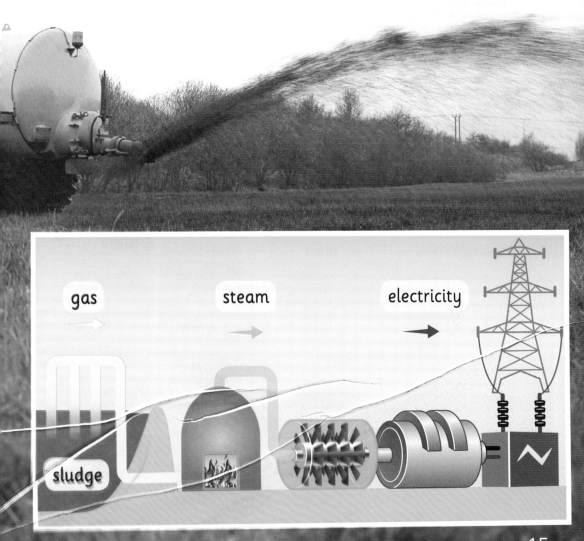

gas   steam   electricity

sludge

Water in our taps

Water companies make sure we have a source of clean water in our houses.

This water technician is measuring the water quality.

Did you know?

River water is cleaned with the same chemical that keeps swimming pools germ free.

Drains: an important invention

Our bodies need water to function properly. We also need water for washing. Thanks to drains, water can be cleaned, recycled and sent back to our taps.

Did you know?

In places where there are no drains, there is often illness and disease.

Wonderful water

Water is necessary for all living things. But there is only a certain amount of water on Earth and we can't make extra. The water on Earth today is the same as the water when Earth first began.

Your water might have once been drunk by a T-Rex!

Hurray for drains!

tap water

sewer

water company

treatment plant

river

23

After reading

Letters and Sounds: Phases 5–6

Word count: 477

Focus phonemes: /n/ kn, gn /sh/ ti, s, ci /s/ c, ce /zh/ s

Common exception words: of, to, the, into, are, once, our, today, water, any, do

Curriculum links: Science: Everyday materials; Design and technology

National Curriculum learning objectives: Reading/word reading: apply phonic knowledge and skills as the route to decode words, read common exception words, noting unusual correspondences between spelling and sound and where these occur in the word; read other words of more than one syllable that contain taught GPCs; Reading/comprehension: develop pleasure in reading, motivation to read, vocabulary and understanding by being encouraged to link what they read or hear to their own experiences

Developing fluency

- Your child may enjoy hearing you read the book.
- Take turns to read a page, encouraging your child to read all the "Did you know?" texts with appropriate intonation for the question and fact.

Phonic practice

- Challenge your child to read the following, listening for the /sh/ and /zh/ sounds:

  sure   measuring   specially   pollution   generation

- Can your child find other words with the "tion" spelling of /sh/? (e.g. *invention, function, medication*)

Extending vocabulary

- Take turns to choose one of the following words and suggest a definition for a glossary:

  special (e.g. *designed for a job; made for a purpose*)

  germs (e.g. *microscopic things that can cause illness*)

  medication (e.g. *pills and liquids given by doctors; drugs that treat illnesses*)

  invention (e.g. *something that hasn't been made before; a new thing someone has created*)

Comprehension

- Turn to pages 22 and 23. Discuss what happens to waste water using the photos as prompts.